Alexandria Township

UNKOSIYAZI

CONTENTS

1   DO I REALLY LOVE   Pg 6

2   TWO SIBLINGS   Pg 15

3   FOR THE KINGDOM   Pg 19

4   RUITS OF MY WOMB   Pg 23

5   ONE NIGHT THRILL   Pg 24

6   TRUTH UNTOLD   Pg 30

DO I REALLY LOVE

As they made their way towards the counter of the Spree Shopping Supermarket situated on the suburbs of Blackheath, Johannesburg; Andrew suddenly noticed that his girlfriend was not with him. He wondered what was going on and where in the hell she had vanished to. He looked left and looked right, he looked down the aisle that was directly opposite the counter, there were still no signs of her sweetheart. He decided to move across the store aisles so that he could see through the aisles that had become barriers in finding that which belonged to him. He passed the first aisle as he moved eastwards inside the Spree Shopping Market and there were no signs of her. He passed the second and third aisle and on the fourth one he spotted three figures with one of them looking like Dudu, his girlfriend. He made his way down the fourth aisle so as to inspect the activities that were taking place behind his back.

Apparently, Dudu had spotted these two figures coming in to the shop as Andrew was still busy boring her by comparing merchandise prices, she recognized one of them as her friend Debra that she used to go to college with. Dudu and Debra attended the nursing college, Ginsberg Hospital College. They were there for three years before Debra got herself expelled from her studies. Debra was expelled after she was found guilty of torturing a patient by leaving an injection needle stuck in his buttocks. The patient was a five-year-old boy that was afraid of getting shots. Debra had lured this poor kid by promising him sweets and juice if he behaved himself. The boy had succumbed to Debra's enticing not knowing what was really in the deal for him. A piece of the needle was left on the boy's left buttock after it had broke as the boy was jumping and prancing around trying to take out the apparatus from his buttocks.
The whole bioscope got aggravated as the student nurses and outpatients left what they were doing and stood and watched this grotesque act, which was perpetuated by Debra. The boy had to be taken to theatre, as they had to surgically operate on him to remove the piece of needle that was stuck on the left chick of his buttocks.

After that incident, the Ginsberg Hospital College officials, Student-Nurse Representative Committee and the local municipality sent Debra packing immediately after an enquiry that was conducted.

Dudu had not seen Debra since then and she was over the moon to see her. As

Andrew got closer, he was shocked to see his girlfriend that she loves so much kissing what at first appeared to be Debra but turned out to be somebody else. It was her ex-boyfriend, Trevor who was looking very feminine. Andrew knew about this guy that Dudu was smooching down. His name was Trevor. Dudu was kissing him on the mouth and he moved his mouth away from her since what Dudu was doing surprised him. Dudu didn't notice the signs of repulsion probably because she was overwhelmed by excitement and joy to see Trevor.

"What the fuck is going on here," furiously asked Andrew.
As he forcibly separated Dudu from the man, he held her on a nasty chokehold as he gave the man a big clap.
'This is none of your business," said Dudu to Andrew as she was coughing after she had managed to free herself from Andrew's tight-gripping chokehold.
Debra did not know what to do or say so she just stood still like a stoned zombie.
"How many times do I have to tell you about this," asked Andrew?
"You know what, I'm sick of you trying to tell me how to run my life, who to love and who to keep as friends. You can't stop me from caring about people, and that goes for Trevor too," she said that as she held Trevor's hand.

Trevor was still perplexed about what had just happened, the clap and the threat from Andrew. Trevor was Dudu's ex-lover of five on-and-off-years. Dudu had only been with Andrew for about four years now.

"But you told me you were over this guy, remember? You told me that he was history to you, remember that," asked Andrew?
"I said it, so what's your point? And besides, that was then and this is now. Some people can and do change their minds."
"Over night," asked Andrew?
"Yes, over night, what's wrong with that? Just because you don't have an interesting life doesn't mean that you should cramp ours, said Dudu.

As they exchanged words, people had stopped what they were doing in the shop and were watching a circus show, courtesy of Andrew and Dudu.

"You know what? I'm out of here," said Andrew as he turned his back from the three of them.
"I told you that I have a soft spot for Trevor," loudly said Dudu so Andrew could hear. Andrew didn't even look back, just kept on walking, spitting fire and

cursing.

Dudu's words reverberated in Andrew's head as he made his way out of Spree Shopping Supermarket leaving everything behind for fate to take care of its own self.

He got on his car and left.

Trevor and Debra apologized to Dudu for putting her into trouble with her man. Dudu told them that they shouldn't, she is a big girl and that she needed to teach Andrew not to be overprotective.

As Andrew drove off from the store he did not know where he was heading to, but he soon found himself traveling down the N1 highway. He started replaying in his mind what had just happened, the words that Dudu spoke as he left the store were ringing in his mind like jingle bells. He asked himself, 'what did Dudu mean when she said that she will always have a soft spot for Trevor?' What is this 'soft spot' stuff about? How can she have a 'soft spot' for Trevor while she is in love with him? How does one develop this 'soft spot'? Do you have to bewitch or charm that individual in such a manner that even if he or she is out of your life, they really never leave but still have that effect as to possess your everyday thoughts, capabilities and dreams? Andrew wished he could get answers to the questions that had suddenly poured down in his mind. He thought of how it would be like to be a female for a day so that he could understand how they think and act and maybe, he'll be able to understand this 'soft spot' rhetoric. What does one do to have someone have a 'soft spot' for him or her? Do you have to be a good kisser, a smooth talker or do you have to be good in bed to earn the 'soft spot' title from your previous lover? Can one have a 'soft spot' for someone without being that close to that person? The more the questions came the more the need for answers grew, but who was to help him solve this 'soft spot' enigma. He didn't know whom to turn to, so he just kept on driving to where his heart was taking him.

Back in the Spree Shopping Supermarket, Dudu and her old friends were happy to see each other. They left the store to a nearby coffee bar to catch up on some lost time over a cup of coffee. The mood was jolly as they sat, drank and reminisced about the past.

"Where have you been and what have you been up to all these years," Dudu sincerely asked Trevor. Before Trevor could answer, Debra interrupted her.

"I thought you were happy to see me too," commented Debra.

"I am my friend but this one," pointing at Trevor, "I haven't seen this one in a long time. We'll catch up my friend at our own pace. Let me attend him first." Debra was disappointed by what Dudu was saying but she didn't show it, she just agreed to what Dudu had suggested.

"I'm going to the restroom, I'll leave you two to catch up because I can see that I'm not welcomed here," she sarcastically commented as she got up from her seat heading to the toilet.

"But you know my friend it's not like that."

"Yeah, yeah, yeah…" said Debra as she walked away.

"So tell me, where have you been hiding," asked Dudu?

"Well, after we broke up or lost contact, I went to London for a year and just did some odd jobs here and there," said Trevor.

Dudu became more intrigued and fascinated about what her 'ex- lover' had been doing since they last saw each other, so she started asking more find-out questions about other things such as his love life. Suddenly, Dudu's questions made Trevor feel uncomfortable since they were about a topic that no longer interested him. Trevor has been struggling with questions like the ones Dudu was asking since he's been back in South Africa, a place that is more homophobic than the one he just came from. Trevor was practicing a new religion and he didn't know how to tell Dudu, solely because she kept on asking all these questions without giving him a chance to say anything. Her questions were innocent, remember that Dudu haven't seen Trevor in ages and all that she wanted was to find out more about him. Trevor decided to do the talking after gathering some courage to do so.

"Listen, I know we haven't seen each other in a very long time. I know that and you know that."

"Yes I do," replied Dudu.

"Well, when I was away in England a lot of things happened there. I had a lot of life changing experiences, and one of those experiences was that I discovered I was drawn or rather attracted to people of my own sex." While Trevor was about to continue talking some more, Dudu interrupted her.

"What? Why? But…" Dudu asked sounding shocked to what she was hearing.

"Let me finish… and please don't ask me why I am what I am. I chose to be what I am and I'm feeling comfortable the way I am," he said sounding agitated a little.

Dudu could not believe what she was hearing, so there and then, she got up and excused herself. She left Trevor seating in the table and Debra while she was doing what ever she was doing in the bathroom that was taking her forever to come out.

On the road, Andrew was listening to SeventeenFM and a song by D'Angelo entitled, "How does it feel" was playing. By this time, Andrew had finally calmed down. He decided to make a u-turn and go back to his townhouse. Andrew and Dudu shared a two-bedroom apartment in Sandton. Andrew was the fortunate one to afford to pay rent.

As the song was playing on the car radio, he thought of how they first met and how sweet and romantic it was. They met four years ago in 1999. A mutual friend introduced them when they were in a 21st birthday party in Mondeo, south-west of Johannesburg. They have been in love ever since, they've had their share of stormy weathers, ups and downs but nothing to make them stop enjoying life. Life is to be enjoyed not endured.

D'Angelo reminded him of their first embrace, first kiss that led them to getting it on that first night they met. Andrew could not forget that night even if he tried to; they both have fruits to show for the labors of that first sight heated passion. It was all history but at that moment in time, Andrew had to revisit it. Suddenly, Andrew snapped out from reminiscing about the past and he tried to focus on the way forward with the matter at hand. He had bills to pay, a four-year old to take care of and a wife-to-be to nurture. There was a lot at stake and he could not afford to mess up.

Andrew was known in the past for being a ladies man, a lot had changed since then, and he had responsibilities and a demanding career. On the other hand, Dudu was an unsophisticated lady, born and raised in Natal. Andrew recalled how when he had gotten Dudu pregnant, he had to pay for the damages he inflicted on her. By the Zulu customary law, a man has to pay a certain number of cows as a fine for impregnating a female he is not married to.

Andrew had also started paying lobola for Dudu about a year ago. Andrew was a circumcised Xhosa man who respected culture and tradition, whether his own or that of others. He was born and raised in Peddie, between Grahamstown and King Williams Town. His parents claim that one of their forefathers fought the British along side Chief Sandile and Chief Maqoma during the Frontier Wars of 1850 and 1870. Andrew was really proud of his ancestral heritage. Andrew graduated the School of Medicine in Unitra with flying colors; he was now running his own private practice in Alexandra Township. The township wasn't his ideal place to work but he had no choice, he had to pay the bills. He wanted to get an office in

Sandton but he was told that there is a six year waiting list. He figured that it was just some bureaucratic procedures made to try and keep the Black man down. It is hard for a black man to follow his dreams the right way in this country.

Dudu had a diploma in Marketing and Management from the renowned AAA College. Even with that diploma in hand, she couldn't secure herself a job. She had decided two years ago that she should go back to the desk and get more education in order to enhance her chances of a dream job. She was studying BComm Economics full-time and did some part-time jobs at Vertigo clothing shop in Sandton Mall and she also did some acting on television commercials. Dudu and Andrew were a young couple trying to make things work in life.

All of this happened about five years ago. A lot has happened since then; Bandile their daughter was in grade three in one of the expensive primary school in Woodmead. Dudu left university after wasting unfruitful three years and then realizing that a BComm wasn't her sort of thing. She was now working in an Advertising Agency as a Marketing Specialist. Andrew had moved to some small office in the city centre of Johannesburg. They had a traditional marriage followed by a white wedding four years ago in Andrew's hometown of Peddie. Dudu was still keeping contact with Trevor behind Andrew's back. Every time Andrew was away attending surgeon's seminars, Dudu would invite Trevor over to cuddle up and keep her occupied. She saw this as a perfect time for them to catch on some lost time. She wasn't doing this with Trevor only, but with other males as well. It's been going on like this for about three years now.
When Dudu and Trevor were going out back in 1998, they never indulged in sexual activities. Some part of Dudu wasn't at peace with the fact that they had never had sexual intercourse.

Before Andrew even met Dudu, just after breaking up with Trevor, she used to hustle her body for day-to-day living essentials, and nobody knew about this. It was kept a secret between her conscious and her heart. Dudu was one of the slickest, slyest, double-timing woman ever to live. Somehow someway she enjoyed being a slut, it gave her a rush and was thrilling to her. Andrew would suspect things now and again but he never really had any strong basis to pin Dudu on, the girl was very slick. Her dubious behavior sprang from not getting enough love, care, attention, and recognition while she was young. She longed to be loved and cared for, through multiple sex partners she felt it was the only way to redeem her lost innocence and make up for what she never had while growing up. Dudu never cared about a damn thing.

Dudu came from a broken home with no mother, and the father she had was very abusive; a drunkard and it is said that he molested her every time he came home drunk. Dudu had a heart that didn't bleed after she had run away from home at the age of eleven to live with her grandmother on her mother's side in Alexandra Township. It is in her grandmother's home where she was taught to uphold her morals. Her grandmother was a firm believer of the Most High who taught her about faith, repentance and about keeping the Lord's commandments. The grandmother's seeds fell on a rock that used to be sedimentary but has become igneous due to the unfair deals life dealt in Natal. Her friends in the township introduced her to lots of bad things. They would get boyfriends that were twice and even thrice their ages when they were still fourteen, fifteen and sixteen, just for money, good times and clothes. Dudu's grandmother was on pension and was supporting three other souls plus Dudu, so Dudu had to do what she had to do to survive her fate. It is here where she was introduced to the business of selling her body for money. All that she did back then sure managed to get her to where she is now.

She tried so hard to kill the habit she had developed in her past but it was hard for her to redeem her innocence. One can argue that she didn't try hard enough, but who are we to judge this young woman. I have heard some go as far as to say, 'once a whore always a whore, no matter what you do to change her she'll never change. It's like Ginger in the movie Casino.' What would you have done if it had been you? Innocence is such an invaluable treasure that should be protected by the cherubim and the flaming sword like they did with the garden of our first parents. Once innocence is gone it is gone forever, you can never buy it or even claim it back.

Trevor never at once fell for Dudu's pernicious seductions; he would refuse to sleep with her when Andrew was away. Trevor did this not just because he was homosexual but also because he never thought it was a right thing for anyone to sleep with another man's wife. He wouldn't like it either if someone was to bone his "husband or wife" behind his "or her" back. Dudu didn't care about not getting it from Trevor because her well of sexual pleasures sprang from different springs, tributaries and streams, which constituted of ex-boyfriends, former customers as well as new found friends.

This pattern continued for some time up until Trevor felt strongly impressed to notify Andrew about Dudu's scandalous behavior. As I said earlier, Andrew always had his doubts about Dudu but he had been ignoring them since he was forever busy trying to improve his professional career. Even his friends had made him aware of what his wife was getting up to when he was away. Andrew had his share of cheating in the marriage but it wasn't out of control like it had lately become with Dudu.

Trevor was the only man that Dudu would bring home to spend time with them, simple because Andrew knew him or about him and Bandile was also accustomed and acquainted to him. Dudu would arrange with her private lovers to meet them in their houses, apartments, lodges and hotels. Old habits die hard.
Andrew cut down from sleeping with his wife, when he did he would use a condom. He probably figured that it was the only way to safeguard himself as well as his interests. One would ask what his interests in a situation like this were.

They had been to all kinds of therapists, traditional seers and healers, counselors, psychiatrists, you name them, they had seen them and nothing helped. Some said that she was probably bewitched into loving men too much. When others would ask where they can find the man that gave her that root, most people were quick to say that the man who can remove the spell on her died a long time ago and nothing could be done.

I guess Andrew was only married to Dudu for two reasons - one was the hope he had that maybe all that Dudu ever wanted was a happy home since she was a product of a broken home - the second was the fact that they had a kid that needed to be raised in a functional family. But Andrew and Dudu were seriously having a dysfunctional marriage, which was hazardous towards Bandile's well-being. Can love withstand all types of weather? For Andrew, love for Dudu had walked out the door. Dudu was under the impression that Andrew was an unfortunate guy that needed to be trapped down. Andrew is the one who paid the rent; put food on the table and clothes on their backs. The money that Dudu made from her part time gigs was spent on clothes and what not.

To cut the story short- Dudu unfortunately had to pay a price for all her late night creeps, cheating and two-timing Andrew and for all that she did. She contracted the HIV virus, got divorced by Andrew, she went and stayed with her decadent grandmother to deteriorate and die there. Andrew re-married; he married a doctor he had met in one of the workshops he attended two years ago. He has two kids from his new wife, a boy (Vusi) and a girl (Nothando). Trevor and Andrew became the best of friends even till today. Bandile is in grade six, Vusi is now three years old and Nothando is a year old.

Dudu died in a hospital where Debra, her best friend was working. Debra was devastated.

TWO SIBLINGS AWAIT THE START OF THEIR FATHER'S FUNERAL

The chapel (church) is packed with all kinds of people. A majority of them are in mourning, and those happen to be females. You know, old church ladies in Africa become animated when it comes to mourning the dead. Their kind of mourning is worn on their faces, the way they walk and the way they talk. On the other hand, the men in this church have red eyes, definitely not from crying (mourning) and not from over-night activities of slaughtering a beast (cow), but from drinking traditional beer. These men still believe that Nguni men must not show his discontent for pain or sorrow. My grandfather used to say that it was feminine for a man to show his tears in times of pain and sorrow.

Anyway, my younger brother and me have been asked by our loving mother to accompany her to attend a funeral of our father, a man we barely knew. My older brother could not come. Matter of fact, my mother refused my older brother to attend the funeral. She said that she did not want to create unnecessary attention and tension when it comes matters of inheritance (will). I am sure my father did not have a will and even if he did, his brothers will definitely execute whatever will is there according to their own tastes and interests. My twenty-two year old brother stayed at home while my seventeen-year old brother, our mother, and me attended the funeral. There is only a two-year age difference between my younger brother and me.

Funny enough, we have not seen this man- our father that is, in almost our entire lives but here we are in a church packed with strangers who knew him but us. Our mother barely talked about him, our grandmother always talked about our father when my older brother was being disorderly.

The church building is small and hot; my mother keeps fanning herself while my younger brother and me wipe sweat of our faces. It is January, the middle of summer, no wonder. In our culture there is a saying that says: "One must wait for the preacher man with a chorus." The females take such saying in to heart as they sing their hearts out. Men and women are on their feet singing and dancing, African style. In the chorus area of the church, just below the pulpit, there is my father's wooden coffin posing as an expensive metallic casket. On top of the coffin there is a photograph of my father with an Afro hairdo. It looks like it was taken back in the '70's. My younger brother keeps staring at the photograph as if he is in conversation with him through it. If I were to write a book about what he is seeing, I will probably title it: PORTRAIT OF A YOUNG MAN ON A COFFIN.

Anyway, like I said, the church is packed and I am feeling uneasy. The reason why I am feeling uneasy is because as a second-born, if my older brother is not here in attendance of the funeral, whoever wants to start nonsense will start with me. So as a grown-young man, it is expected of me to defend my mother and my younger brother from any anything that might go down, unexpectedly. I do not anticipate anything funny to happen but as I keep looking around the church room, I keep seeing funny faces and I keep telling myself that they are not funny but they are unfamiliar. It is the faces I have never seen before. It seems as if they are also carefully observing how my mother is behaving. Our mother chose for us to seat in the middle of the church. Customarily, we were supposed to sit in front next to all the relatives instead of mixing ourselves with strangers. Kin or no kin, our mother told us before we even left home what we needed to do and say. We were briefed before we even arrived at church. Even on our way there, she kept testing our memory if we still remembered that we were not supposed to talk to any one, and where we were supposed to sit and all.

I do not like funerals, ever since my grandmother passed away; I developed uneasiness for funerals, worst of all for strangers such as my father. My younger brother persuaded me two days ago to go and pay my last respects to the man who fathered me. He called it, closure. Out of respect and lack of desire for arguing, I agreed to go with them. I remember saying to him that I do not need closure because I never knew the man anyway. That did not go down well with both my brothers.

On top of the coffin there is a writhe together with some other flower arrangements, cards with condolences messages. The tenor and base from the men is making the roof tremble as they sing *Rock of Ages*:

> Rock of Ages, cleft for me,
> Let me hide myself in thee;
> Let the water and the blood,
> From thy wounded side which flowed,
> Be of sin the double cure;
> Save from wrath and make me pure.
>
> Not the labors of my hands
> Can fulfill thy law's commands;
> Could my zeal no respite know,
> Could my tears forever flow,
> All for sin could not atone;
> Thou must save, and thou alone.
>
> Nothing in my hand I bring,
> Simply to the cross I cling;
> Naked, come to thee for dress;
> Helpless, look to thee for grace;
> Foul, I to the fountain fly;
> Wash me, Savior, or I die.
>
> While I draw this fleeting breath,
> When mine eyes shall close in death,
> When I soar to worlds unknown,
> See thee on thy judgment throne,
> Rock of Ages, cleft for me,
> Let me hide myself in thee.

My father was a Lutheran and apparently this melancholy hymn *Rock of Ages* was his favorite hymn the times when he really felt like being church (spiritual). Strange enough, it was when he was intoxicated that he felt spiritual. My mother tells us. It is funny that such news one has to hear them during *el día de los muertos* (funeral). The moment the song finishes, everybody sits down. Everybody is dripping wet with sweat and it is not even funny. Worse of all, the funeral has not even started yet.

Few seconds later, the Choir Conductor walks to the pulpit (podium) and asks the congregation to rise to make way for the Reverend, and to sing our father's favorite hymn, again. The keyboard starts playing *Rock of Ages* slowly and it crescendos as the congregation catches on with it. The Conductor is also animated by now. As I look behind me, I see a big, fat Reverend dressed in a black gown decorated with crosses of red and green. The Reverend is followed by a stream of men that are dressed in gowns of all colors. It looks like it is going to be a long funeral. Now I wish for that *Rock of Ages* where I can hide myself from this agony.

TO BE CONTINUED…

FOR THE KINGDOM

Then shall the kingdom of heaven be likened unto ten virgins, which took their lamps, and went forth to meet the bridegroom...

For the kingdom of my husband (and Lord) can be likened unto the women (ten wives) that his ancestors gave to him.

And five of them were wise, and five were foolish...

But his ancestors knew what they were doing because they had instructed the husband to take these women into marriage so they can beget sons and daughters for them. Mind you that these children are or were not for the husband and his wives, but they were or are for the husband's departed grandmothers (ancestors).

They that were foolish took their lamps, and took no oil with them: But the wise took oil in their vessels with their lamps...

The foolish wives did not take good and sound advice from their elders at home, they were the rebellious type and the sensual type whom always to prove they were right even when they were wrong. The fact is, they were foolish and they knew it but their stubbornness blinded them from acknowledging the fact. Instead of them doing as they were instructed by their mothers and fathers, they did as they pleased.

The parents said: "Uyokuvova umendo."

The community said: "Hamba juba bayokuchutha phambili."

Others said: "Isalakutshelwa sibonwa ngomopho."

The wise wives took advice and counsel from their parents. These wives had respect. They were taught respect. They were taught love. They were taught honor. They practiced all of these things at home before they were given by their fathers to their husband (and Lord). These wise women were wise - nothing more and nothing less. Hands make a man, and these wise wives respected and loved the gift of work, they were not lazy and they were virtuous - compared to the foolish wives. The Old Ones of our Tribes believe that everyone can be taught and everyone can learn, it is up to that individual to then choose to have such education liberating or enslaving (burdening) him or her. They believe that a man (husband) doesn't need to love his women but it is his duty from the gods and God to bear children for his ancestors and to teach them the ways of the Tribes and to offer sacrifices for the ancestors (gods) so that when he is gone (they have taken him back to them), the children will continue the traditions of their father(s). And that is why happy is the man who has his quiver full of them for he shall not fear when he meets his enemies by the gate. Keep the spirit of your ancestors alive through cows and goats, please!

While the bridegroom tarried, they all slumbered and slept...

The husband was on a hunt, which was called by his ancestors. The husband was on a far away country taking care of his businesses and affairs so that his loved ones might be well (taken care of). While the husband was away, the wives became restless, emotional, lonely and hot-blooded even more. The foolish ones started flirting with other men and doing and saying all types of things that showed disrespect towards their Lord (husband). The wise ones (wives) even thought they were sad, lonely and love-sick, they had virtue and honor because they were taught (raised) well at home. The wise wives could abide.

And at midnight there was a cry made, Behold, the bridegroom cometh; go ye out to meet him...

The husband was gone for a long time and just like any other man who goes on a hunt - he doesn't know when exactly he will be back home again. All that he knows is that one day he will be back because even a man that once abandoned his homestead will one day return. Besides, even if he didn't want to - the gods will make him return. Who will do the ceremonies for them if he doesn't return? Who will guide, teach, admonish and raise the children in the ways of his (their) forefathers? But the wives did not know when their Lord (and husband) will return, so when a call was made that they should go and meet him - it came as a surprise to all of them.

Then all those virgins arose, and trimmed their lamps...

They were surprised and happy that their husband (and Lord) has finally come so they made themselves ready and look presentable for their Lord (and husband).

And the foolish said unto the wise, Give us of your oil; for our lamps are gone out. But the wise answered, saying, Not so; lest there be not enough for us and you: but go ye rather to them that sell, and buy for yourselves...

But the foolish wives who were mischievous while their husband (and Lord) was gone wanted the wise wives who had honor and respect for their husband (and Lord), to give them of their virtue, which they so abundantly possessed. But the wise wives told the foolish wives that they will NOT do so for they all had time to learn to be virtuous, respectful and to have honour. Besides, how does one give virtue (chastity) to an immoral as if they were exchanging goods for money? The foolish wives had wasted their time and energy quarreling, carnal and being disrespectful when they were being taught to honour and respect their elders so that their days may be long on earth. The wise wives were wise - the foolish wives were fools. Virtue is not something you share or give to those who don't have it. Virtue is earned. There is a price to be paid for virtue. That is why that things like love, respect, honour must be taught from an early age at home so that when the time comes, the wife will be able to respect her husband (and Lord) if, and only if she fails to love him. Respect is greater than Love. For her - she has to respect the things of her husband's ancestors. She must remember that the ancestors of her husband (and Lord) have given her to him to help him fulfill his duties and callings. Not everyone is made for marriage, not everyone is made for polygamy, so choose carefully and make informed decisions before you find yourself feeling trapped. Divorce should only be reserved for adultery, frigidity, and sexual perversion.

And while they went to buy, the bridegroom came; and they that were ready went in with him to the marriage: and the door was shut...

On the 25th hour where can one buy or get virtue (oil to keep her lamp going) as the wise wives had suggested that the foolish wives do? For when the husband (and Lord) came to take his wives to the love-mat that night, not all were ready. The foolish wives were not ready (ashamed) because they could not (abide) keep their virtue, honor and respect for their husband (and Lord). Who are we fooling? The foolish wives had none of the above. The foolish wives went home to consult with their mothers or their family's ancestors but what good was it for because the door was already locked. The husband (and Lord) had already welcomed the Chosen Ones. Remember, many are called but the chosen are few.

Afterward came also the other virgins, saying, Lord, Lord, open to us. But he answered and said, Verily I say unto you, I know you not...

After the advice and counsel they have gotten from their friends, family and magazines on how to treat their husband (and Lord), and how to be virtuous - it was sad to see that it would have been well with them had they had taken time to learn these things from those that were willing to teach them to them. Now when the husband (and Lord) divorces them, what are they going to do? Go home and bother their parents? Be on their own (single)? For how long? Remember that the children belong to the ancestors of their husband (and Lord)! Some of them had children with their husband (and Lord) already. Now which man was going to rescue them? If they had failed on keeping their marriage at first what are the chances that they were going to keep it this time around when they find another husband? Well, there are no guarantees, in life (love) we take our chances - maybe the foolish wives (ex-wives) will find marriage. Unless if it is true that once a fool always a fool. The foolish ex-wives must remember that the children must remain with the husband (and Lord), they were and are not for her. At least now they will be raised and under the care of the wise wives. These are the wives who have paid the price for the ticket to the kingdom of their husband (and Lord). The wise wives could abide, and they did. They were raised well and even though they had their times of trial (test) they always remembered the things they were taught at home - love, honor, and respect. They came prepared for anything and everything. We should thank their parents for the good work they did because these are the women we need who are going to leave footprints (wisdom) for our young ones and those yet unborn, to follow. They are the shining examples of womanhood.

Watch therefore, for ye know neither the day nor the hour wherein the Son of man cometh...

FRUITS OF MY WOMB

To many women it is given the eggs to be fertilized by semen so that procreation may happen. But to many women - it is not given. So those that have the eggs (talents), let them use them, to fertilize them so that children for our ancestors may get a chance to come to earth and partake. Let us not be selfish and say that it is too costly nowadays to have children. We can't put prices on the heads. Life is worth much more than gold. For as long as we have the land, the gods and God will never let us starve and die.

We are the children of a Higher God. So women - use those talents that the gods and God have given you to help Him in his Plan of Creation - you are a Creator too, remember that and respect it. Don't let those eggs (talents) go into waste every month because some of you go through a painful period when the egg doesn't get fertilized.

A time will come when you can't make babies anymore or when you have made already enough babies for the ancestors of your husband (and Lord), but up until then - fulfill your duty and calling. For unto every one that hath shall be given, and he (she) shall have abundance: but from him (her) that hath not shall be taken away even that which he hath.

ONE NIGHT THRILL

It was during summer, on a Friday afternoon about two years ago, Bongani was busy delivering pizzas when his cellular phone rang. Usually, on Friday's he would finish attending his classes at 12:00 and would go to work for about five hours at most. On the other hand of the phone was his friend from university telling him that he needed him to come to university as soon as he could and that it was very urgent. He agreed but told him that he had to get permission from his 'no-nonsense' uncle to use his car. When he got home from work, he asked his uncle and fortunate enough, his uncle concurred to his request but admonished him to make sure that the car was in the garage by midnight. He agreed.

"The car needs to be serviced and I am going to do it first thing in the morning. I have already bought the oil, petrol and air filter, fan belt, oil, shock absorbers, brake pads and brake fluid", he said as Bongani was changing from his work clothes to street clothes.

Off he went to meet his friend, Blessing at the university residence, he had been waiting for him with four other guys for about an hour and they were drinking booze and puffing weed. When he got there, what Blessing said to be of urgency during his phone call was after all, about pursuit of sexual pleasures. Blessing told Bongani that they needed him to help them with an extra car to go pick up some girls in Pretoria to a party he was organizing that evening. Apparently, Blessing's parents were away for the weekend and that called for a house party. What Bongani was hearing sounded so good and he was impressed by what was in it for him especially since it has been ages since he had something, something. He told them his situation about his uncle, the car and all. They understood. As the sunset, phone calls were made and targets were located.

With their hormones raging, they raced their way to Tshwane in two cars to pick up about five girls that one of them guys had organized. They were there in 15 minutes and to their uttermost disappointment, the girls were with their 'significant others'. It turned out that there had been a misunderstanding between the girls and the guy that knows them. The girls were under the impression that they were coming to pay them a visit. They went outside to the parking lot and phone calls were made quick and one guy contacted some prospective targets in Hillbrow, Jozi. Again, they raced their way down to Hillbrow to pick up the girls. It seemed like these girls had been waiting for them to call (to get picked up to any party, anyway) them. The ratio was 6:5 (six females to five males) and that was pleasing to them because it meant that there was enough to feed the needy and there was no need to be greedy. They were so excited by now to find girls who were so reciprocal to their intents.

Time by now was 21:00; money was collected to buy last minute booze (liquor), meat, rolls and snacks for the party. The girls were looking salacious and Bongani was looking forward to what the young night had in store for him. His intentions was to take the girls to the party house, get recompensed and try to beat the midnight hour as his uncle was such a strict man. He did not want his uncle to loose trust in him by disobeying his command. He definitely did not want to ruin his chances of ever being loaned the car.

Apparently, three of the guys had been imbibing some intoxicants as well as abusing pharmaceutical extractions. By now they were a bit rowdy and Blessing tried to keep them in control. Bongani told me that he tried taking some few puffs of weed as peer pressure had gotten hold of him, but he choked from it and stopped there and then. "Screw trying to fit in, I must just concentrate on driving and staying drug free" he told himself.

When they got all that they wanted for the party, they drove to Blessing's house in the eastern suburbs of Jozi. Again, they were speeding but this time Bongani did not have any intentions of being the fastest. Blessing had said:

"Please bro! Follow us so that you don't get lost since you are not familiar with the directions of where we are going to."

"Don't worry bro, I got you", he said.

So he followed them.

Music was blasting off the car speakers, four girls plus one guy who were in his car were singing their hearts out to the music. It was crazy. Beer cans and Jack Daniels bottles were passing and weed smoke was in the air. The girl that Bongani was feeling was seated in the front seat and he could tell by the way she was acting that she was really feeling him. That gave him more courage to act like 'Boet Madlisa'. He could imagine by then in his mind what a stupendous party these people were going to have because the girl's omens of being reciprocal to their enticing were evidential. He felt so bad about it all because he knew he had a curfew he was not intending to disobey. The car he was driving was a 325is BMW, 1988 model and it was in satisfactory running condition. It had lapsed his memory for a moment that the car had a history of performing unexpectedly when put under pressure. To make matters scarier was the fact that the car was three weeks late for service though his uncle was planning to do it the day after that Friday. Bongani's uncle was a DIY (Do It Yourself) man, he believed in doing things himself.

As they were pulling up the driveway of the house, the car started doing some jerking moves and he looked on the temperature gage/ gauge and the car was overheating. He managed to drive it all the way to the carport, right by the light before it even stalled.

"Damn man! This can not be bloody' happening" he cursed out loudly for everyone to notice his frustrations.

He knew then that his 'so promising night' had to be sacrificed soon if he wanted to be in good terms with his uncle.

As I had mentioned before Bongani even got to these mess, his intentions were not to stay until morning. He had planned to drop the girls and boys by the house, stay for a minute or two and maybe get in to some action with this one honey that he was feeling- and go. By now, all of that was no longer in his mind. Time by now was about 23:14 and all he wanted to do was to find and fix whatever was faulty with the car and leave. He thought of letting his uncle know about what has befallen him but sooner realized that telling him was like committing suicide. He was going to be in some serious shit with him because he did not tell him he was going to pick up girls in his car. He had told his uncle that he was going to a casting agency for some casting, which was a lie.

Two guys offered to help him while the other two were entertaining and playing host to the ladies. Apparently, the fan belt came out and that is why the car was overheating.

They struggled to get it back in order but could not. He could not call for a mechanic because he knew that those cost an arm and a leg. They tried and tried and an hour passed by, still they could not manage to get fan belt fixed. It is about 31 miles away from his home and where the party was. He wished for a miracle but knew that the only miracle that was going to happen had to performed by him, by getting himself and the car home before his uncle suspects his absence. It must have been about 00:23 when he decided to bid the boys and girls farewell and try to get home before 'shit hits the fan'.

Off he drove trying to get home before 01:00 at least; he would drive for about a mile and a half and fill up some water on the cooler (radiator). After driving for about 10 minutes on the highway, the car finally stopped functioning and the battery went flat. He managed to pull over the side of the road safely and he just parked there hoping for a serious miracle to change his ordeal into joy. At about 01:28, he saw some lights flashing on his rearview mirror and a taxi pulled up behind him and two middle- aged men came out and walked towards his car. One of them had a flash light (torch) with him.

"I was scared the hell out of myself because I thought that I was getting hijacked." He later told me.

"Howzit my friend?" asked one of them.

"I'm fine".

"What seems to be the problem?" asked the other one.

"My fan belt came out and the car would not start", he said.

They told him to open the hood of the car so they could see what was wrong. He opened it.

"What are you going to do? We do not have our tools with us but we can tow you to our place, try and fix your fan belt, alternator or what ever is wrong in your car", suggested one of them.

He asked them if they could tow him home, but they refused saying that it was way too far for them.

Having no option, he allowed them to tow him to Alexandria. Alexandria Township is perceived as being the most notorious and dangerous township in South Africa, I am not so sure about that myself. In general, townships are good residential areas with decent citizens residing in them. Some are not though, so was the case with Alexandria, so I thought. Bongani had never been to Alexandria and had never intended to do so but little did he know that fate would lead him there.

"I did not know whether I was going to be helped or killed upon getting there. As they were towing me, I wrote an sms on my cellular phone telling my girlfriend that I was being towed to Alexandria township in case I was not going to make it out of there. I also gave her the registration number of the taxi that was towing me. I could visualize them killing me, making the news on the morning broadcast and my family burying me and me having even got a chance to achieve things I wanted to achieve. I was feeling fury for my so-called friend (Blessing) for neglecting me in my time of want" he told me after a week of his ordeal had passed.

They arrived where the two- men stayed; they lived in a well-congested shack community. People were up and down the streets at 02:00 in the morning. Bongani was scared to death and thinking of the stories he heard and read of people being murdered and never found. He thought he was going to add to those statistics. They parked and they started working on the car. Anyway, it turned out that the assumed devil was a saint after all. These guys were innocent taxi drivers/ owners with families and they were coming from their rank in Johannesburg city when they stumbled upon him. It took them about an hour to get the fan belt fixed; he had been anxiously saying his silent prayers for the car to get sorted out before break-of-dawn.

Luckily, he had made about R150 from delivering pizzas plus R50 that the guys gave him for gas. He was able to pay these ghetto 'angels' for rescuing him. He paid them R200 as a token of appreciation and of good neighbourly love. They were kind enough to show him out of the Alexandria maze (township streets) to the highway. They exchanged numbers and promised to keep in touch. He was amazed and shaken up as he drove he made his way home. On the way he was asking himself why did he get in and out of this situation that he just came from? He was not looking for answers, these were just soul searching questions on himself. He rolled the car in the garage and managed to sneak in his room at about 03:30 without waking up any one. It took him forever to fall asleep, his pillows were wet from tears of overjoyed for making it home safely mixed with tears of pain what had happened. By the time he fell asleep he told himself that he would never allow himself to be used by fake friends like that anymore… WHAT A NIGHT!

TRUTH UNTOLD

A car stopped and a window rolled down right next to where Jabu was walking. She wondered who the hell it was and what the hell he wanted!

It was in the early hours of a hot and sunny- summer afternoon in Johannesburg city center. Jabu was walking on the left hand side of Commissioner Street when the car pulled up next to her. Jabu had just finished attending her computer classes in one of the Secretarial Colleges on DeKorte Street, Braamfontein. She was on her way to Jeppe hostel to pay her uncle a friendly visit. She had been asked by her mother to stop by her uncle's place and get umuthi wokuchatha and intelezi to steam up with and nokuphalaza.

"Where are you going to sweet lady," asked the stranger? Jabu acts as if she didn't hear him but she replies anyway.

"So that," responded Jabu?

"I just want to meet you, you know," he said looking at her in the eyes?

"Well- you've met me and besides, I don't talk to strangers," said Jabu as she was walking, still puzzled by what this man was saying. The man kept on driving and stopping so as to keep up with Jabu's pace.

"They say a stranger is a friend not met yet, so let me park there and then I can walk you to where you going," said the man soon after he had spotted an open parking lot in front of him.

The stranger parked his car with the help of a car guard. The car guard whistles as he directs the stranger's car maneuver so that he could park safely in a parking lot that had just opened up.

"My awthi, please look after my car, okay," the stranger begged the car guard that looked like he had just emerged from a coal mine chimney.

"Me take care for your car big boss, nee worry sy kaar is baie safe with me" said a toothless car guard in his broken English, trying to assure the man's car safety. The car guard whistled as he did some foot-stepping dance moves with excitement and hopes that he will get a nice contribution from the man when he comes back. The car guard was thinking that the driver was a rich man judging from the wheels he was pushing. Johannesburg is a city built on gold. It is here that people from all over South Africa and neighboring countries come in search for gold- their dreams. In Johannesburg and especially in the city, you need someone to look after your parked car because anything can happen while gone. Someone can break in, steal what is inside or outside or even steal the damn car. So the car guards come handy even though you can never fully depend on them. Most of the car guards are homeless people, beggars and the jobless who decided to create jobs for themselves by guarding parked cars.

When all of this was happening, Jabu did not bother about waiting for the stranger to park the car. She was almost half a block away from where she first encountered the stranger. In her mind she was thinking about what this stranger wanted and about the distance she still had to walk to her uncle's place.

"Catching a ride with him to Jeppe hostel on a sun- scorching day like this won't hurt," she thought.

"But how can I let him take me there? What would he think if I tell him I'm going to a hostel? No I won't do that," she reasoned with herself.

A girl like Jabu had to be conscious of what kind of places she goes to. She can not afford to be spotted in a male hostel, what would she say she was doing there if someone that she knows was to see her?

"No, no, no, and definitely a big no. I have to uphold my reputation," she said.

If it was not for her grandmother, there was no way she was going to be caught dead in that hellhole. Hostels are normally filthy places, which houses men who work in mines or railway roads and industrial areas. These are men who were once conscripted to come and work for a minimum wage in the city. Though I still wonder if these people are still being underpaid for the hard work they do. Hostels are neglected by the municipality and they are very unhygienic for any human being to live in. Most of these men in these hostels come from rural areas and some do not know better but where they come from is sure better then being in a hostel.

"I'm Thabo from Rossetenville by the Turffontein Racetrack," he introduced himself as he finally caught up with Jabu. Rossetenville is on the southern suburbs of Greater Johannesburg.

"I'm a motor mechanic by profession and a handyman by work," said Thabo in an assuring voice.

"What do you mean you are a handyman," Jabu asked with signs of concern upon Thabo's mentioning of the word 'handyman'?"

"I work with my hands to do and fix things," he said.

"What kind of things do you fix?" She posed a follow up question.

"Why are you so interested in what I do? I work with my hands and that's all that matters. Besides, we shouldn't be talking about me, but about you. So tell me-Uyaphi, uphumaphi and what do you do? Do you work, study or what?"

Thabo changed the order of questioning. It was him now who was doing all the questioning.

"I work in some office in Braamfontein…, I'm kidding. Actually, I'm taking some computer classes at BESC," she said.

"What does BESC stands for?"

"Braamfontein Elite Secretarial College," replied Jabu.

"Okay," Thabo nodded.

There was a moment of silence for about a second or two, and then Thabo broke the silence by asking Jabu where she was going? She thought of telling 'the stranger' the truth but then decided to do otherwise. She told him that she was meeting someone by the Carlton Centre Mall.

People were walking up and down, cars and taxis making a lot of noise, the city center was busy. Thabo was having a hard time trying to keep up with Jabu and to communicate freely without any disturbances.

"Who is it?" He asked.

"It's none of your business!" She rudely replied.

"That's rude," commented Thabo.

"That's the way you look at it. Anyway, let me go, it was nice meeting you," she said.

"Not so fast," he holds her hand so that she wouldn't walk away. They are now standing in front of Carlton Centre Mall.

"Lahlela amadigits akho khona ngizokuthinta sometime," asked Thabo?

"What is it that you can't say now that you have to call me for?" She asked with signs of irritation on her face.

"Don't get me wrong sweetness, just wanna keep in touch. I mean, you are nice, your style is killing me and I just wanna see you again," he said in a begging mode.

"Let go off my hand then. Anyway, I do not have a cell phone and even if I did, I wasn't going to give you my numbers because I don't give away my numbers to strangers," she smiles afterwards.

"I'll give you my friend's number if that's okay with you," she looked him in the eye.

"I'll appreciate that but is your friend always with you," Thabo asked as if she can tell that Jabu was bluffing him.

"Sho!" said Jabu.

Okay, ithini then?"

"0, 8…" Thabo interrupted her as he was still taking his Siemens out of his pocket.

"0, 8 and what," he asked as he enters the digits in his cellular?

"0, 8, 4, 7, 8, 2, 6, 4, 7, 7, her name is Kedibone. Thabo stored the numbers on his mobile and he promised to keep in touch. He asked Jabu if he can call her later on that night and she told him that he should call during the day and when it is school time.

As they went different ways, Thabo could not contain his excitement for being able to get Jabu's contact numbers even though they were her friend's, he did not mind. Suddenly, a thought came to his mind:

"Lenkwamba nje maybe idlala ngami. I know she has a cell phone.

Kubukeka engathi kuyalahla nje! I'm going to call her.

Upakishe kamnandi umntwana wabantu, ngingey'tholele yena nje madoda ngimuthi, mfimfithi."

As Thabo was thinking all of this, Jabu was crisscrossing her way through the mall to Main Street to catch a taxi to Denver.

"Where is this man that's supposed to be looking after my car? Maybe I have a parking ticket already," he wondered as he went to check the front of the car.

"Ngamla van my, yonke into imnandi. Bafikile ohrata and ngakulahlelela ipondo. U-ankela ukugadele kahle itrans yakho. Awumzame ngento esile ngamla," begged the car guard as he smooth-talked Thabo. By the time the car guard got done with his soliloquy, Thabo was already inside his car, backing up. He maneuvered his way out of the parking bay leaving the man begging for 'mercy' with his hands together in a cupping shape.

"This man is drunk, I had only been away for three minutes and he tells me ospeed kop bafikile. Ubhem'igudu," he said as he drove off.

As Thabo drove away, Jabu was already in a taxi to see her uncle to pick up what her grandmother asked her to get. She was thinking about what had just happened as she journeyed to Jeppe hostel.

"What did Thabo mean when he said that he was a handyman?

Was that his car? He has a nice car if it is his!

Does he really stay in Rosettonville or Rosettonville was the only name he could think of?

Will he call?

I wonder what he wants.

He is cute but what if looks are deceiving me? We'll see because it's not like he is the first ukung'shela. But what if he is different from the rest? Maybe he is a nice guy. Guys are all the same anyway, just dogs that just want to use us and string us to their convenience. No one will use this girl. Over my dead body.

Damn, it's hot today and my periods are killing me," she said as she was about to jump off from the skorokoro taxi she was riding.

When Jabu arrived at her uncle's hostel room, she found him busy meshing some herbs on a mortar with a wooden spatula. The door was wide open. The man saw Jabu's shadow engulfing the door and he looked up.

"Kwilanga elishisa kangaka, ubekwa yini kulelizwe lethu ngane kadadewethu," asked a man who was in his late fifties?

"Grandmother sent me to get the usual stuff," she him a piece of paper.

"Are your neighbors still bewitching my sister's house," he asked?

"Yes."

"Mhh, kanti banjani abantu? Bayokuyeka nini ukuthakathana bodwa. Even kuleSouth Africa entsha abantu abamnyama basacekelana bodwa phansi. Kwenzenjani kodwa emhlabeni," he commented as he looked through his mortar as if looking for answers to his questions. He stood up and offered Jabu his seat. Jabu sat down as her uncle went to another room with a list that Jabu had just given him.

Few minutes later, the old man came out with some parcels wrapped up with newspaper and he hand them over to Jabu. Jabu puts them inside her school bag.

"Kuyaphaseka eskoleni? Wenza ubani manje," he asked?

"I'm studying computers," she said.

"Kwakuhle lokho ntombazane, ufunde uzimisele. Remember that in this great future, without education yabelungu, awuy'lutho. Education is your PASS to a better job, opportunities and a better and long life. This PASS is different from the once they use to make us carry back in the days. This one doesn't expire, it is yours forever. Children today need to use the opportunities they get to better equip themselves with life skills, knowledge and wisdom." By the time the old man finished lecturing Jabu, she was already standing up getting ready to leave. She gives him R30 and bids him farewell.

Jabu was a curious sixteen-year-old girl going for seventeen in two month's time.

She was a very pretty girl and very bright. She had a body of a twenty-five year old and she was middle height, light in complexion with an Afro hair-do, which complimented her long facial features similar to those on Picasso's Les Demoiselles de'Avignon figures, though she was not primitive but she was more towards modernity. She had a beautiful and a seductive smile. She had an hourglass figure, compactable ass with well- rounded hips- a typical African mama.

Her legs were straight, long and well built. Her morals were not questionable at all, so untypical of township girls who are known for being scandalous at times. Most people, especially men would mistake her for a slut just because of how she looked, walked, talked, dressed and her attitude. Older men are the ones who always made advances at her but she would not give them any time of the day. Thabo must have been lucky that she even got her friend's contact details.

Jabu came from a very poor family, she had a mentally handicapped brother and her grandmother was on a pension fund. Her grandmother's pension money and her younger brother's disability grant are what brought food to the table, clothes on their backs and a roof over their heads. But that did not stop Jabu from walking with her head up high. It never bothered her that her mother and father perished from AIDS- related deaths when her younger brother was still eight, about five years ago. Their grandmother took the initiative of raising them when no one was willing to assume the responsibility of caring for them, especially for a retarded boy.

A day passed, two days, three days, a week passed and Jabu had forgotten about the man she had met about a week ago. Thabo didn't keep his promise to call Jabu. In fact, not too long after about a month or so later to be precise, Jabu and her two friends were at Ubuzekezeke Nightclub on some false identity since they were minors to go clubbing. The club scene was dry and they were bored to death and about to leave when at 00:38, she felt a tap on her shoulder and as she turned over to see who it was, to her uttermost surprise, it was Thabo. They were both happy to see each other. He told her that he had tried several times to contact her but the number she gave him was either busy or off every time he tried it. They 'figuratively' kissed and made up since all he was saying was all in the past and it was all blue lies. They were happy that fate had led them to meet again in such an environment. They exchanged phone numbers. Thabo was happy for the opportunity that has presented itself for he was going to catch up with her on some lost time. Thabo introduced the friends he was with and Jabu did the same. They drank, talked and danced the night away. Thabo bought them drinks, rounds after rounds. Thabo acted like a gentleman. Jabu and her friends were very impressed by his manners.

Jabu noticed that something was strange on Thabo's face; he had acquired a bad scar under his left jaw, close to his neck.

"What happened to your neck?" Jabu asked after repeating her question for the third time. Trying to talk to some one in a nightclub can be a hassle unless you scream your lungs out that is what she was doing so that Thabo could hear her.

"I was in a car accident about three weeks ago," he said. Somehow Jabu did not buy what Thabo was saying. To her it looked like he got the scar from something else other then being in a car accident. What it was that he was hiding, she knew that sooner or later she had to find out. Time must have been around 03:15 when Ntsindiso (one of Jabu's friends) suddenly suggested that they leave the club as soon as possible. Jabu and Tumi (the other girl) seconded her motion after a long time of persuasion by Ntsindiso.

As they walked down the Jorisen Street away from the club, they started arguing about why they had to leave when they were still having a time of their lives. Ntsindiso told them that she recognizes the face of one of Thabo's friend; she had seen him on television and newspapers. He was wanted by authorities for a Durban Foreign Exchange outlet robbery about three weeks ago. She told them that Thabo's friends were acting funny and she did not feel comfortable being there. They looked like they were up to no good. The girls dismissed Ntsindiso's accusations and told her that she was probably mistaking the guy with someone else, or maybe she was not seeing properly because of having too much to drink. They argued this all the way to Tumi's little apartment where they were going to be sleeping. Jabu had asked her grandmother to spend a night over at Tumi's flat. Tumi was Jabu's friend from back home in Tsakane, a township on the East Rand of Johannesburg. Ntsindiso was from another province, Kokstad in the Eastern Cape. Tumi and Ntsindiso attended the same Advertising College in Rosebank.

Somehow Tumi did not buy what Ntsindiso was saying, she knew that Ntsindiso was up to something. Ntsindiso was known for being amorously attracted to people of her sex. Tumi recalled how Ntsindiso normally acted when she was around Jabu and that always bothered her.

As they were making their way up the old-rusty stairways of D'Urban Court, for that is what the building was called, Tumi was busy pondering what had been said and done these last few hours up until now. Their building was situated on the corner of De Beers Street and Stiemens Street, Braamfontien. Tumi tried to recall what Ntsindiso had said that led them to their bailing out of the club that it didn't make sense to her. Tumi read between the lines that Ntsindiso was up to some thing reprehensible.

"Something has to be done. There is no way that my friend is going to be sodomized by Ntsindiso. I'll rather prefer that she sleeps with Thabo rather then with another girl," she thought as she was also wondering about the sleeping arrangements when they get upstairs. She didn't know what to do but to pray for a miracle. She needed to come up with a plan soon. Tumi had a single bed in her room and Ntsindiso had a double.

Back in the club, Thabo and his two accomplices (Madoda and Ntonto) were kicking themselves, asking why they let their fishes go when they had them in their hands. They were drinking and letting the good times roll. What else could they have done with their money other then to drink, spend it on girls and on clothes?

"Guys, guys, we can't let these girls eat our hard- earned money like that and run away," commented Madoda.

"I'm trying to win her heart man," said Thabo.

"You should be trying to screw her not spending money on her. Don't you know that a way to a women's heart is through her legs," asked Ntonto?

"Kudliwa imali kudliwa umuntu, that's all I'm saying," says Madoda.

"Gents, I hear what you're saying but I'm going to handle this my way," says Thabo as he sounds aggravated.

"That's fine with us, but what about her friends," asked Ntonto?

"Don't ask me. It seems that they weren't feeling you guys coz if they were, they would still be here. And anyway, I'm leaving this place. It's dry now," says Thabo.

"I'm going to buy my good times in Hillbrow," says Ntonto.

"Me too, my baby's mama is gone for the weekend and that calls for a celebration, says Madoda.

"You guys should be ashamed of yourselves, chasing Jezebels and bringing all kinds of diseases to your loved ones," comments Thabo as he gets up from his seat.

"Only if you knew, prostitutes are the least people that are affected by AIDS because they make sure they use protection. If they don't, they die and they can't be in business any more," comments Ntonto.

"Rubbish, what you are saying is what I call amasimba," Thabo walks away from her friends. The way Thabo walked away leaving his friends behind, you could tell that he had a lot in his mind. As he walked out of the club, he was scrolling his cell phone book list for numbers to call.

As the girls enter the flat, Ntsindiso see a bicycle that belongs to Tumi's boyfriend. Tumi quickly goes to her room and she finds her boyfriend fast asleep in her bed.

"I'm doomed," she said to herself as she came out of her room and entered the kitchen. She offers the girls some tea and coffee. Tumi knew that all that she was hoping to avoid was now definitely inevitable to avoid especially since now there was her boyfriend in the bed.

"Can I move my boyfriend out of the bed? But I need to get my groove on and my man won't allow that. But what about Jabu, can I let Jabu sleep on the floor in my room? That is another impossible mission because her boyfriend won't feel comfortable with that idea. Damn, what's a girl to do in a situation like this," she asked herself as she prepared to serve tea and coffee to Jabu and Ntsindiso.

A phone rang, it was Jabu's phone. She wondered who that was calling her at that time of the night. The screen caller ID said: 'Caller Unknown.' Jabu went to the toilet room to answer her phone. While Jabu was gone, Ntsindiso thought it was appropriate to ask Tumi about the sleeping arrangements. She suggested that Jabu sleeps in her room seeing that Tumi had an unexpected visitor. As Tumi was about to answer her, Jabu came out smiling from the toilet room.

"Who was it," asked Tumi?

"Thabo," said Jabu as she was smiling uncontrollable. Tumi could not believe what she was hearing and so it was with Ntsindiso. Finally, Tumi was going to have a peaceful sleep and Ntsindiso on the other hand was going to have a miserable one. But what did Thabo want from Jabu?

"He wants to see me; he is on his way here. I gave him the directions," said Jabu as she tried to sip her tea. A miracle that Tumi hoped for finally happened. Tumi was the first who suggested that she should go with Thabo, Ntsindiso did not like that at all, but she had no choice. Whatever motives Ntsindiso had, they were ruined by Thabo's phone call. I guess we can say that Jabu escaped from the mouth of a crocodile.

Thabo took Jabu to an Inn somewhere in Johannesburg and they spent a sexless night there. She told him that she was still a virgin and was not intending to change it. Thabo did not believe it but he respected her decision.

Thabo and Jabu went out on date after date since the night they met in a club, which was four weeks ago. They were better acquainted by now, though Jabu felt like there were things that Thabo was hiding from her. But by now, Jabu was Thabo's inamorata.

Thabo was 25 years old, he was tall and handsome. He was an easy going type of guy. Thabo was a person who only answered what he was asked at that particular time. The rest of the time he kept to himself. They say you must always be weary of such people because you may never know what they might be up to. So it was with Jabu, she always wondered about what Thabo might be up to. All questions and doubts about what it is that Thabo did for work and more were soon laid to rest when he took her out to celebrate her birthday, which was going to be on a Sunday. What Jabu didn't know was that Thabo had other girlfriends on the side that he was sleeping with while he was still waiting for that day when Jabu would finally 'break him off'.

Thabo was going to be away for the weekend, so they had to dine on a Friday. That evening, they went to a restaurant at Gold Reef City. Gold Reef City is a theme park situated in what use to be a gold mine, which is now inactive due to some flooding that, occurred in some of the shafts.

"Why can't you be with me on my birthday on Sunday?" she asked furiously.

"I have to take care of some business. I have to be in Bloemfontein," he said.

Jabu didn't like that they had to go and celebrate before her actual birth day but it happened that during their dinner at the Grace restaurant in Gold Reef City, Jabu managed to have her concerns she has been having for nearly two months, resolved.

"Kahle, kahle, wenzani for work?" Jabu asked curiously.

"Can we talk about that after dinner? I'm trying to enjoy the food here," he said as he reclined back on his chair.

They enjoyed their three-course meal. During the meals though, he kept on getting phone calls that would last for about five seconds at most. It bothered Jabu but she tried not to let it get into her head.

After dining, Thabo quickly suggested that they drive to a house party that he had been invited to in Kagiso. Jabu didn't want to go but Thabo persuaded her until she succumbed. The moment they arrived in the township, Thabo was very quick at suggesting that they park some where and continue. She didn't oppose that idea. They found an isolated spot that use to be a soccer field; it was also a path for people coming from the train station to residential houses. Kagiso is a small township compared to big townships such as the nearby Soweto, and Umlazi in Durban, and Mdantsane in East London as well as Khayelitsha in Cape Town though it is bigger than Alexandra. Kagiso is a warm and welcoming township with friendly people. That is why Thabo decided to take an advantage of its hospitality. Few minutes after they had parked, Thabo suggested that they sit at the backseat of his Jeep. They did and Thabo opened the sunroof so that they could wish upon a star.

As they sat next to each other, Thabo finally told Jabu that he works with cars, meaning that he helps car thieves get buyers for their stolen merchandise. He told her that he is also involved in some money laundering schemes. She was shocked but yet, she expected such an answer.

"How come you never told me this all along? Why were you hiding it from me," she asked?

"I don't feel comfortable discussing what I do with people and that is why I never told you about it before. I also have to carry a gun for protection just incase," he said.

"But I thought I was your girl," Jabu asked.

"You're my girl for sure, it's just that I don't mix business with pleasure," he sarcastically said so.

"What is that supposed to mean," she asked.

"Exactly," he said as he quickly changed the topic.

"As I was saying..," he told her that a man in his line of work needed to stay protected at all times. Jabu wasn't interested at what he was trying to explain, so she looked the other way. Thabo drew her close to him and held her tight in his arms. The moon was full and they were staring at it and Thabo was whispering 'sweet nothings' to her ear and that made her forget about what she had just heard.

Maybe love forgets what is irrelevant or maybe Jabu did not want to spoil their perfect evening? I do not know but what is to be must be.

He was nibbling at her ears and they were kissing and fondling. He put his right hand under her Vera Wang dress that Thabo bought her for birthday three days ago.

"Please don't do that," she said.

"Why not?"

She told him that she was not feeling comfortable about the whole thing. He assured her that she must not worry and that he had everything under control. As he was kissing and feeling her body, from nowhere, Thabo suddenly told her that he was sick and tired of her pushing her away every time he wants to do her.

"Your virgin bullshit stories are making me sick. I want it and I want it now," he said as he ripped her Vera Wang apart by force. They wrestled and wrestled until Thabo overpowered her.

Jabu could not believe what was happening in front of her eyes, how a man she once thought was her 'cutie' had quickly transformed to being a 'beast' in a matter of seconds. Thabo forced himself inside her; she screamed and felt like dying.

In her mind she remembered the thoughts she once had when she was once sitting in a taxi going to her uncle's place in Jeppe:

"I wonder what he wants.

He is cute but what if looks are deceiving me? We'll see because it's not like he is the first ukung'shela. But what if he is different from the rest? Maybe he is a nice guy. Guys are all the same anyway, just dogs that just want to use us and string us to their convenience. No one will use this girl. Over my dead body."

She literally felt like dying as Thabo was raping her. Jabu was struggling trying to free herself from the monster, or from this bad dream she was having. Her evening was blacker than the color black. She remembered the day they lowered both her parents to the ground. She saw herself being laid to rest in a coffin after suffering and dying from AIDS.

"This is not happening," she told herself as she tried so hard to alarm anyone who might have been in the vicinity. Thabo threatened her with a firearm and raped her and told her to keep quiet so as not to cause a scene for passers- by. Jabu thought of a way she could redeem her stolen virginity, her stolen innocence, her stolen integrity, her stolen youth, and her stolen dreams, by the man she thought she loved. It is absolutely true when they say that like a dream, things are not what they seem.

As Thabo was raping Jabu, somehow someway Jabu managed to grab the pistol. They struggled for it for a minute or two and a shot went off and the 'the man', 'the stranger', 'Mr. Lover', 'cutie' was hit three times in the face. Thabo died right on the spot, inside his fleshy Jeep.

Two young men were walking by on the path coming from a soccer training, heard Jabu screams as well as the three shots that went off. They went near the car and instead of offering help; they dragged out Jabu as well as the body of the deceased and took flight with the Jeep and the murder weapon.

Jabu was left on her own to await the arrival of the police. After taking their own time, they arrived as the crowd of people had so quickly gathered around. The police came, they covered the body of the deceased, they asked around for any witnesses and nobody was willing to be of help. Jabu was still very much shocked and traumatized about what had just happened, first she get raped by the man she thought she loved, she kills him in self defense and the car she was in get stolen by thugs. A thought came to her mind: "Who can you trust in this day and age? What happened to ubuntu? Have the hearts of men become that cold?"

The police took Jabu to a nearby Leratong Hospital where the doctor confirmed after examining her that she had been raped. The doctor took some blood samples so that they could do HIV test and other related tests.

Apparently, Thabo had told himself that he had to get sex from Jabu that night no matter what. His patience on her had finally run out, little did he knew that it was going to be him who was going to wind up dead. Thabo was going out of town to meet with members of the Feranji-gang for some Foreign Exchange outlet robbery that he was involved in which went sour about three weeks ago. He knew that chances of him making it back alive from their meeting were close to nothing. Little did he know that things were going to end up the way they did. It is funny how things work themselves out sometime!

THE END